Paul Bunyan

retold by Carol Ottolenghi   illustrated by Steve Haefele

Copyright © 2004 McGraw-Hill Children's Publishing. Published by Brighter Child, an imprint of McGraw-Hill Children's Publishing, a Division of The McGraw-Hill Companies. Send all inquiries to: McGraw-Hill Children's Publishing, 8787 Orion Place, Columbus, Ohio 43240-4027. Made in the USA.   ISBN 0-7696-3283-1   1 2 3 4 5 6 7 8 9 PHXBK 09 08 07 06 05 04

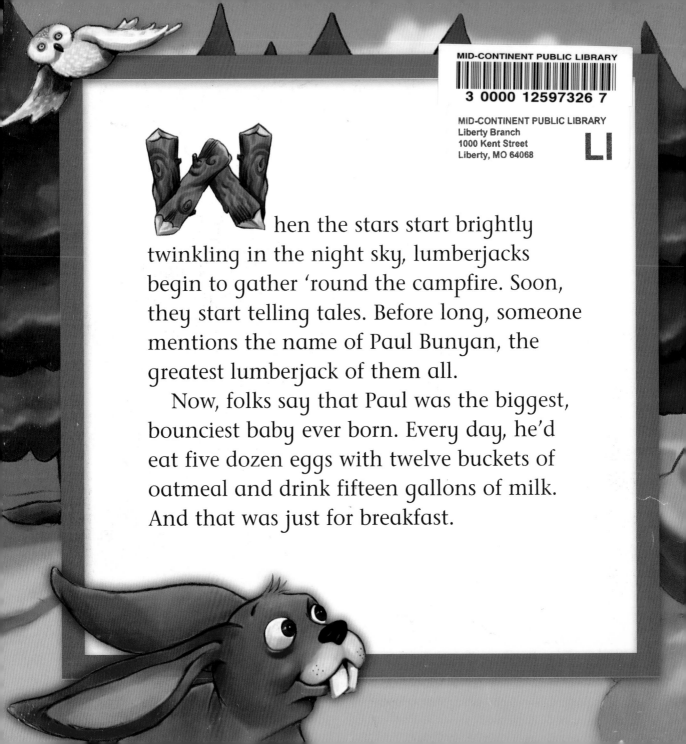

When the stars start brightly twinkling in the night sky, lumberjacks begin to gather 'round the campfire. Soon, they start telling tales. Before long, someone mentions the name of Paul Bunyan, the greatest lumberjack of them all.

Now, folks say that Paul was the biggest, bounciest baby ever born. Every day, he'd eat five dozen eggs with twelve buckets of oatmeal and drink fifteen gallons of milk. And that was just for breakfast.

Paul grew mighty fast. By the time he was twelve, he was taller than his folks' house. Why, he was so big that he used a small pine tree for a toothbrush. And all the ladies of the town would have to knit for one week solid just to make him a pair of socks. I guess that's why Paul's Ma gave him such a sharp talking-to when she heard that he used his sock as a fishing net.

When Paul was old enough, he set off to explore the forests that covered the land. One day, he was caught in a snowstorm. Now, normally, this would have been no big deal. Paul had been caught in plenty of snowstorms. But this snowstorm was different. It was so cold that the snow turned a beautiful robin's egg blue!

Paul tramped through the fluffy blue stuff. Suddenly, he saw a tail sticking out of a snowdrift. Paul pulled on the tail, and out popped a big baby ox!

That poor baby ox was so cold that it had turned blue, too. Paul bundled it up and carried it to a nearby cave.

Paul decided to take a break from his exploring. He set up housekeeping in the cave until the baby ox got better. No one knows exactly where Paul's cave was, but it had a smooth, sandy floor. A little creek ran through the back of the cave, full of cold water and plenty of wriggling fish to eat.

The baby ox grew and grew. Paul got tired of calling it "baby ox," so he shortened its name to Babe.

Babe's name was the only short thing about that ox. It was forty-two ax handles high. No one could guess how much it weighed, but when Babe ran, the ground thundered so loud that folks ran for their umbrellas.

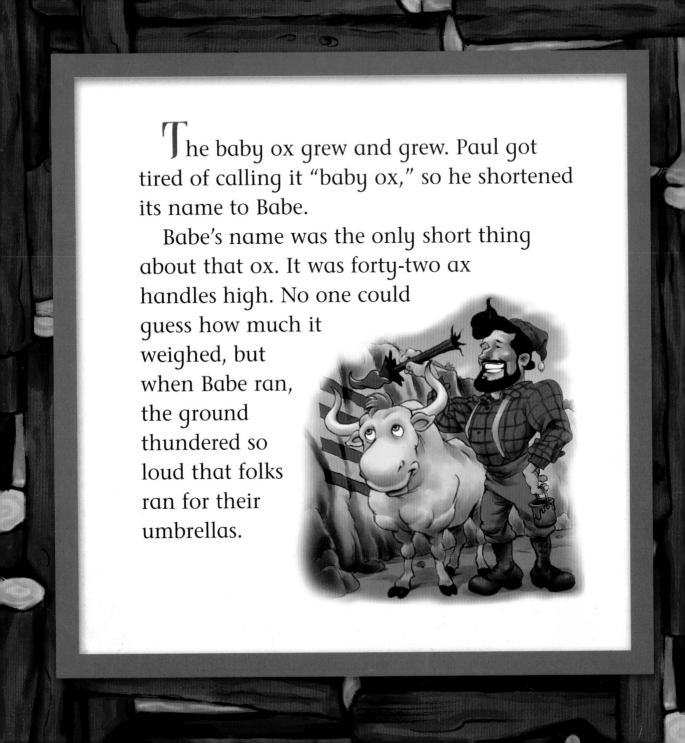

Paul and Babe tramped through the woods. Back then, the forests were as thick and crowded as the bristles on a hairbrush. But that was quickly changing.

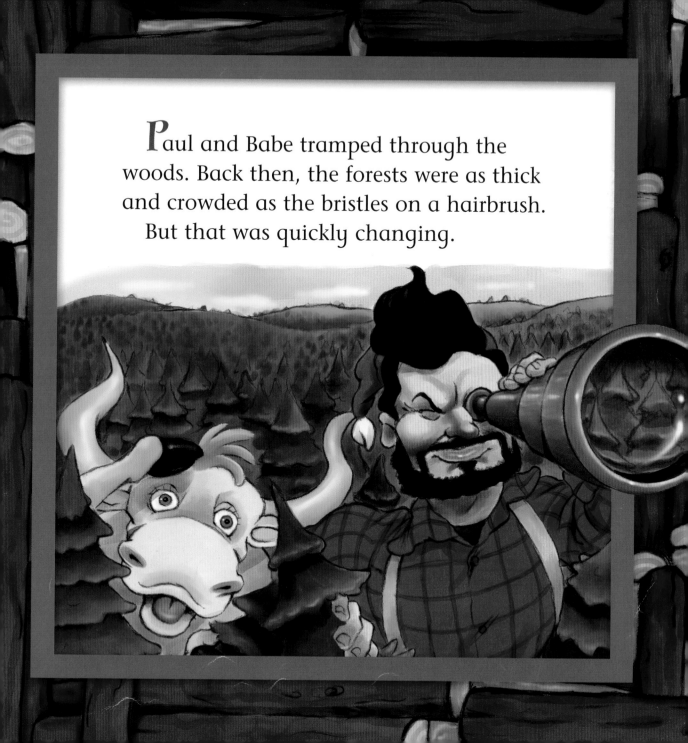

Pioneers were headed west. They built barns and houses and wagons and all sorts of other things. That meant they needed wood.

Paul became a lumberjack. Every time he swung his ax, ten trees would fall.

Paul piled the logs onto Babe's back to take to the sawmill.

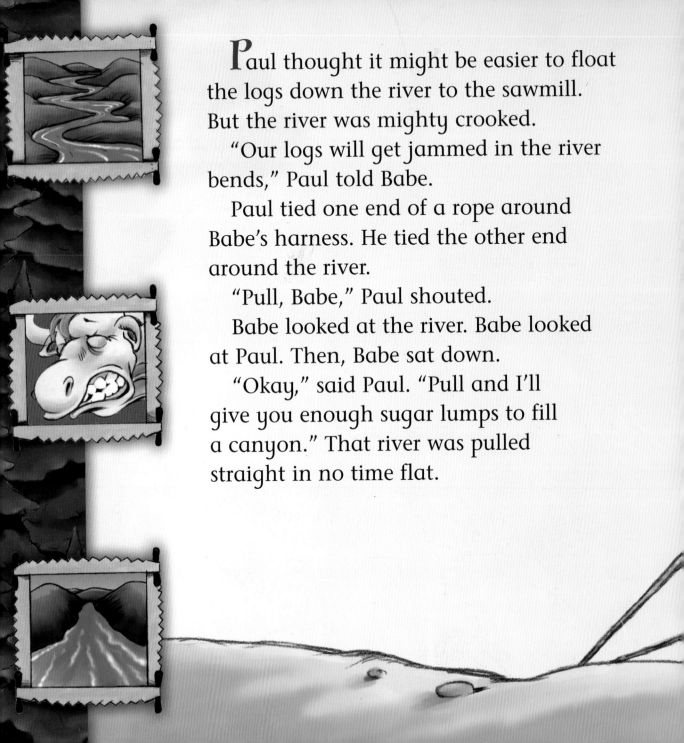

Paul thought it might be easier to float the logs down the river to the sawmill. But the river was mighty crooked.

"Our logs will get jammed in the river bends," Paul told Babe.

Paul tied one end of a rope around Babe's harness. He tied the other end around the river.

"Pull, Babe," Paul shouted.

Babe looked at the river. Babe looked at Paul. Then, Babe sat down.

"Okay," said Paul. "Pull and I'll give you enough sugar lumps to fill a canyon." That river was pulled straight in no time flat.

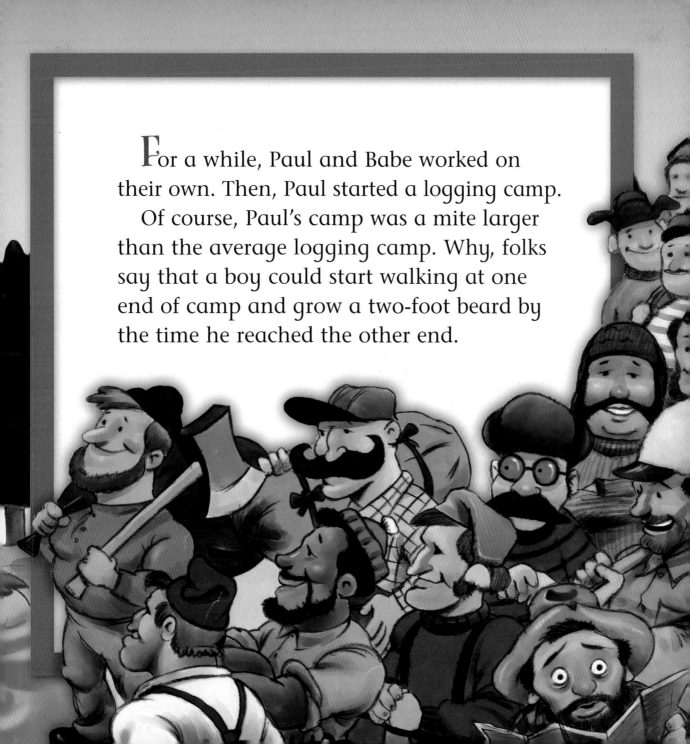

For a while, Paul and Babe worked on their own. Then, Paul started a logging camp. Of course, Paul's camp was a mite larger than the average logging camp. Why, folks say that a boy could start walking at one end of camp and grow a two-foot beard by the time he reached the other end.

Naturally, the camp needed ponds for drinking water. So, Paul and Babe dug the Great Lakes.

Sourdough Sam was the head cook at the camp. He made flapjacks, stew, fried chicken, and spinach casserole. The loggers hated spinach casserole. But when Sam changed its name to "muscle-maker spinach casserole," they ate it up. Every bit.

Yes, indeed, Sam was a mighty good cook. His flapjacks were fabulous. Every morning, the kitchen staff strapped bacon to their feet. They'd skate on a griddle as big as an ice-skating rink. When the griddle was greased up, Sam poured the flapjacks. He used a crane to flip them over.

All the loggers loved Sam's flapjacks, but Johnny Inkslinger loved them most of all. Johnny was the camp's bookkeeper. He paid all the bills and kept track of things for Paul.

Johnny wrote so fast and so much that he had to connect his pen to an ink lake. To save ink, he stopped dotting his *i*'s and crossing his *t*'s. That saved five hundred barrels of ink every week.

Things went pretty well at the camp for a while. But then came the Year of the Two Winters. First, it got cold. Then, it got colder.

Shot Gunderson, the camp foreman, had all sorts of problems. He rode in to chew them over with Paul.

"Boss," Shot said to Paul, "it's so cold out there in the woods that our feet are freezing off. We have to do something."

Paul was big and strong, and he was also clever.

"Tell everyone to grow their whiskers. When their beards get long enough, they can tuck them into their boots. That'll keep their toes toasty."

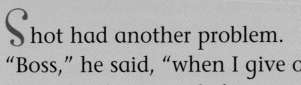

Shot had another problem.

"Boss," he said, "when I give orders or the loggers yell 'Timber!' our words freeze into icicles. No one can hear anything that anyone says."

"Well, I'll ask Babe to haul all the words to one place," Paul said. "When they thaw in the spring, you'll be able to hear what everyone said."

YAHOO!

TIMBER!

CHOW TIME!

TAKE A BATH!

TIMBER!

That wasn't one of Paul's best ideas. You see, all the words thawed at the same time. So, it seemed like folks were yelling all sorts of different things at once. It got a tad bit confusing.

After that cold, cold winter, Paul and the rest of the loggers were ready for a change. They took the logging camp out on the road. Babe pulled the camp along behind them.

Paul and his crew logged in North Dakota, South Dakota, Washington, Oregon, and all points in between. For a while, Paul dragged his ax behind him 'cause it was resting sort of heavy on his shoulder. But he stopped when he realized the ax was digging a trench in the earth. Today, we call that trench the *Grand Canyon*.

Yep, Paul logged a lot of land. But he knew that the trees were precious, so he always left some standing.

Paul got older. He could still log better than any lumberjack alive, but he decided to retire.

One day, Paul and Babe just wandered off. No one knows exactly where they went. Some folks say they headed to Alaska. Others say they went back to their sandy cave. Nobody knows.

But if you keep your eyes open, some day you just might meet the greatest lumberjack ever born.

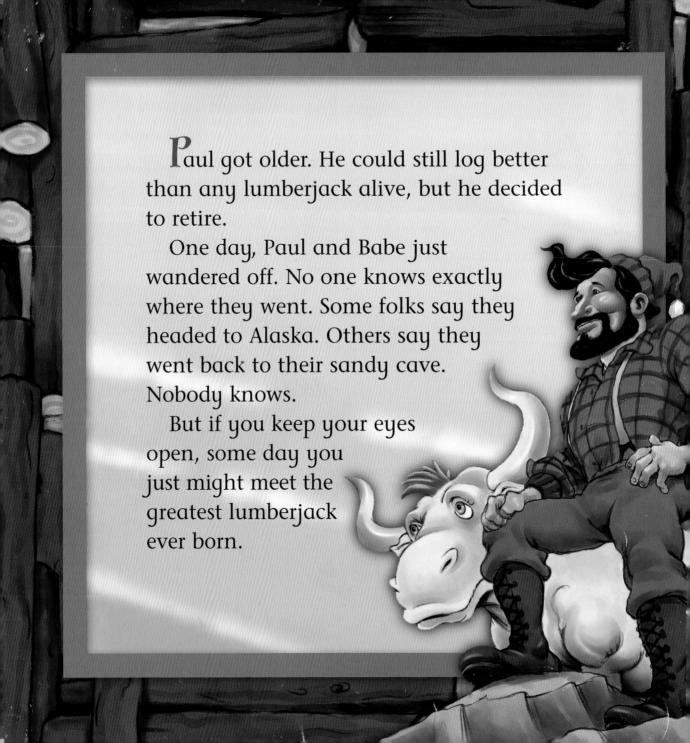